For my brother Shawn, who has ever been brave enough—love, your big Sis

To Joel and Emmanuel—Y

Published by Tradewind Books in Canada and the UK in 2012
Text copyright © 2012 Sheree Fitch Illustrations copyright © 2012 Yayo
Published in the USA in 2013

LIBRARY AND ARCHIVES CANADA CATALOGUING IN PUBLICATION

Fitch, Sheree
    Night sky wheel ride / Sheree Fitch.

Poems.
ISBN 978-1-896580-67-8

    1. Children's poetry, Canadian (English). 2. Ferris
wheels--Juvenile poetry. I. Title.

PS8561.I86N53 2012   jC811'.6   C2012-900647-5

Cataloguing and publication data available from the British Library

Book design by Elisa Gutiérrez

This book is set in Cassia.
Title is set in Liam.

10 9 8 7 6 5 4 3 2

Printed in Malaysia in March 2013 by TWP Sdn Bhd
on FSC ® certified paper using vegetable-based inks.

The publisher thanks the Government of Canada and Canadian Heritage
for their financial support through the Canada Council for the Arts, the
Canada Book Fund and Livres Canada Books. The publisher also thanks
the Government of the Province of British Columbia for the financial support it has given through the Book Publishing Tax Credit program and the
British Columbia Arts Council.

Canada Council   Conseil des Arts
for the Arts   du Canada

BRITISH
COLUMBIA
ARTS COUNCIL

MIX
Paper from
responsible sources
FSC
www.fsc.org
FSC® C106048

Night Sky Wheel Ride

Sheree Fitch

illustrated by Yayo

Tradewind Books

Vancouver • London

Nighttime falls on the fairgrounds
Dark's glitter sparks a dare

Are we big enough this year, Mama?
Are we brave enough, Brother?
Sister, are you ready to fly?

Standing in line
we wait wait wait
At last we're the ones
at the front of the gate

Are we big enough this year, Mama?
Are we brave enough, Brother?
Sister, are you ready to fly?

First stop—
cotton candy shop
round round round
a sugar cloud's spun
melts sticky quick
on the tips of our tongues

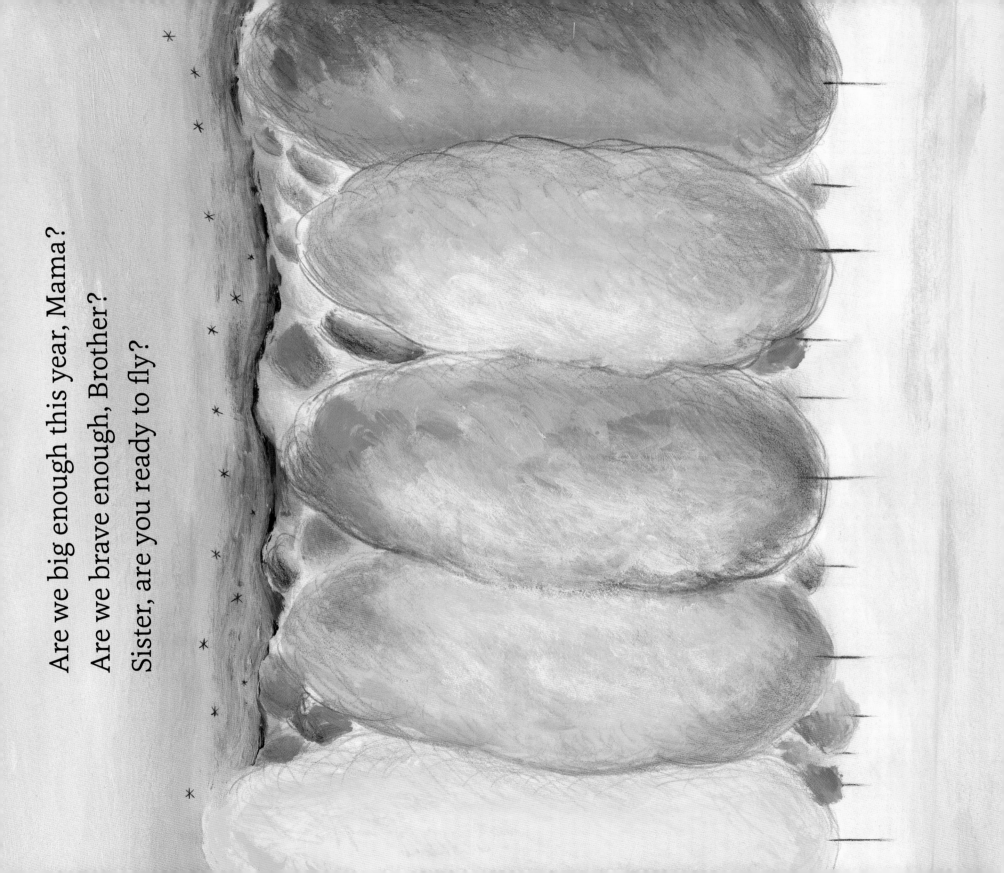

Are we big enough this year, Mama?
Are we brave enough, Brother?
Sister, are you ready to fly?

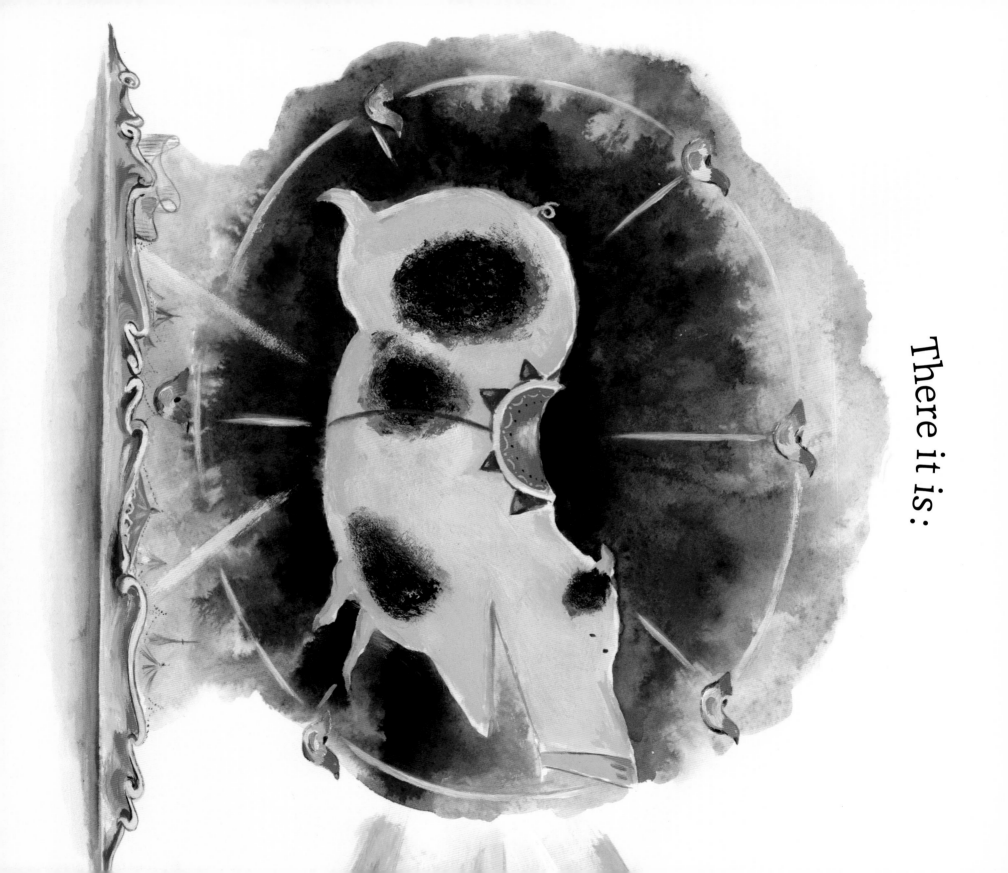

There it is:

The wheeeeeel!

The wheeeeel!

The whirling wheeeeel!

The squeeeeeealing wheel!

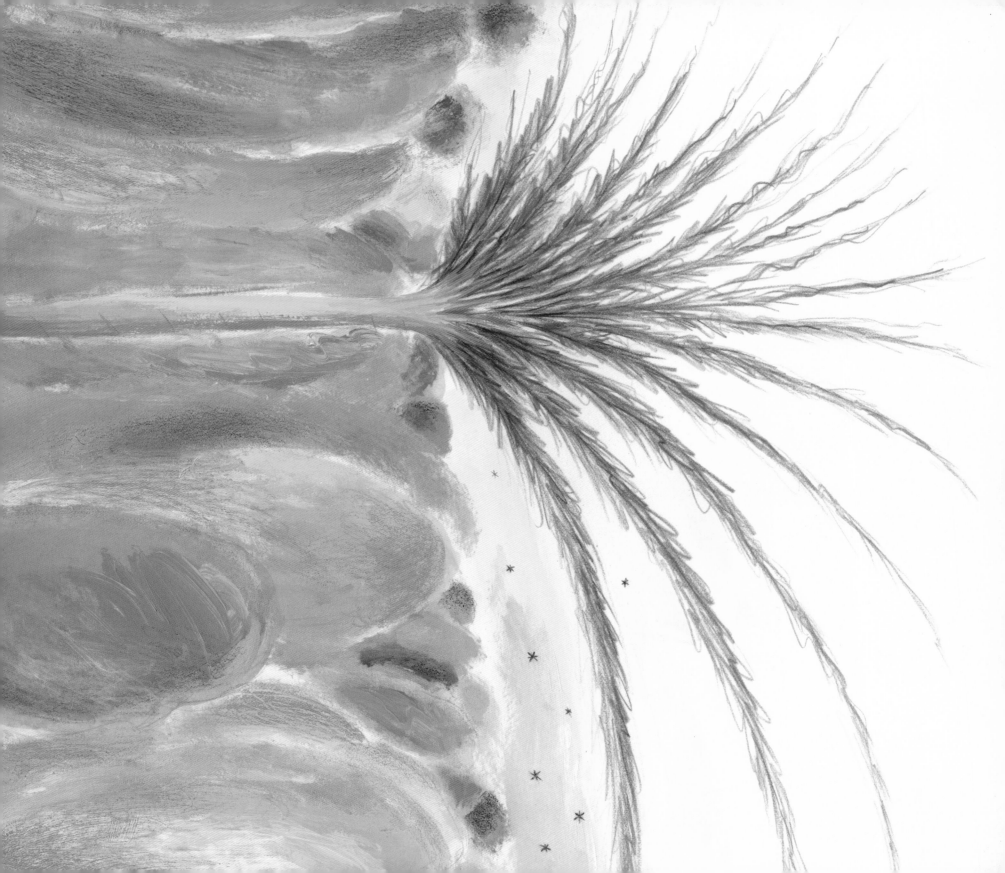

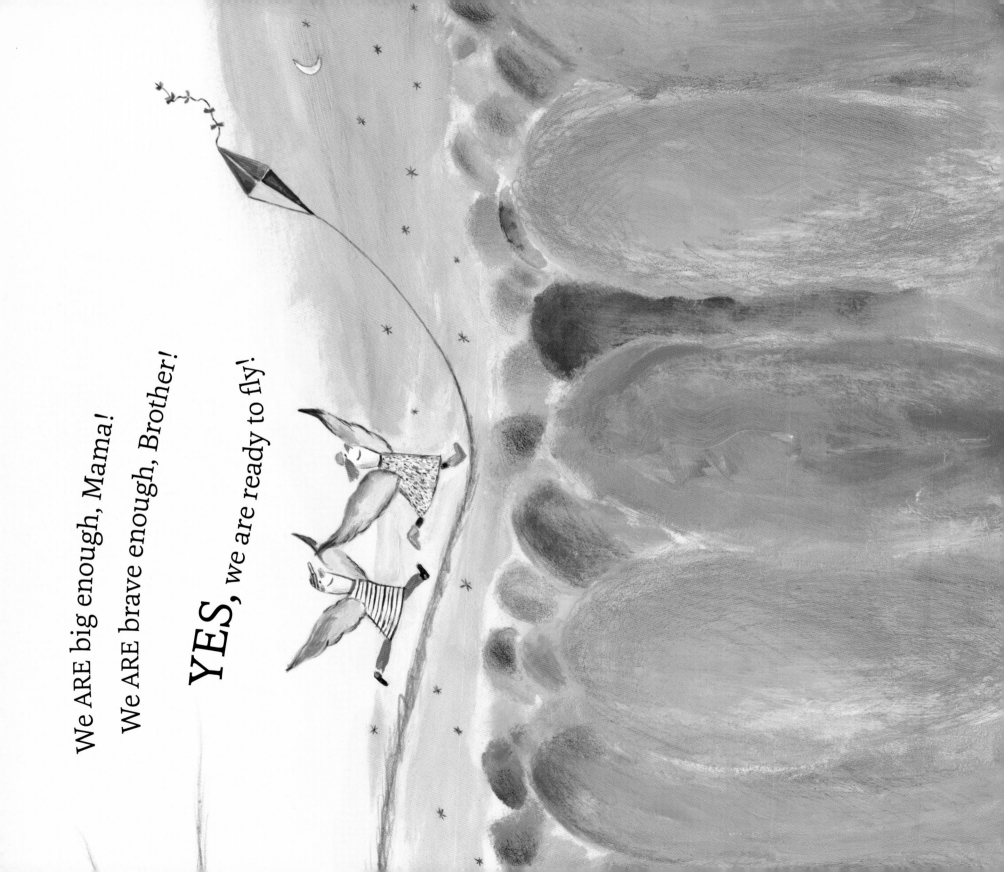

We ARE big enough, Mama!

We ARE brave enough, Brother!

YES, we are ready to fly!

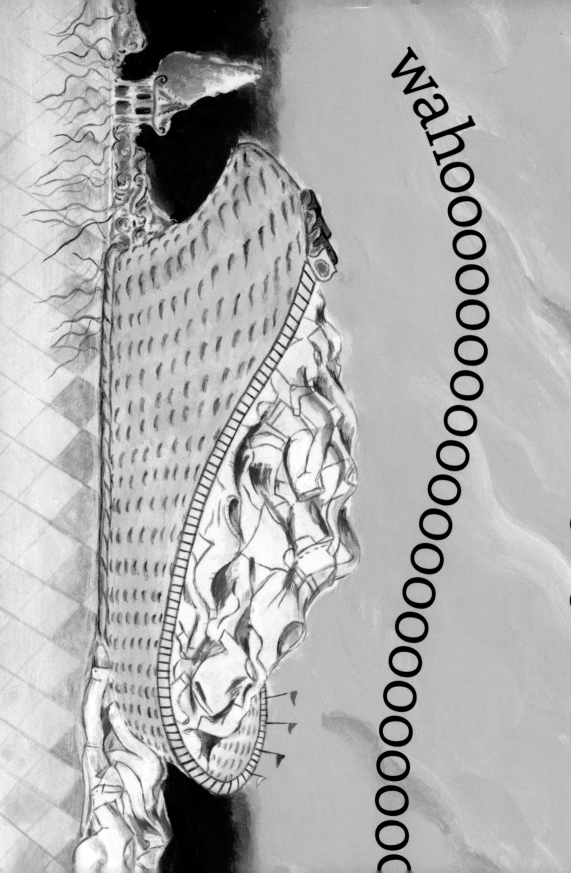

wahoooooooooooooooooooooooooooooooooooooo

Let the spinning begin!

Uh . . . one . . .
uh . . . two . . . .
uh . . . whoopeedeedoo

ride
wheel
wild
night's
Up—down—inside

upside
downside
hang on tight now

Wow!

Then STOP!
Swinging swaying staying
up top
the stopped Ferris wheel
Dizzy-dazed we gaze up
feel the moon's breath on our faces
soft as dandelion fuzz

No! Don't look down.

Not yet, Brother!

Let's play a game
of dot to dot
with Orion's stars instead

See out to sea, Sister.

Hushshsh

hshshhhhhhhhhh

Can you hear the mermaids murmur
beluga whales sing
feel the whirling stir
of every little humming phosphorescent thing?

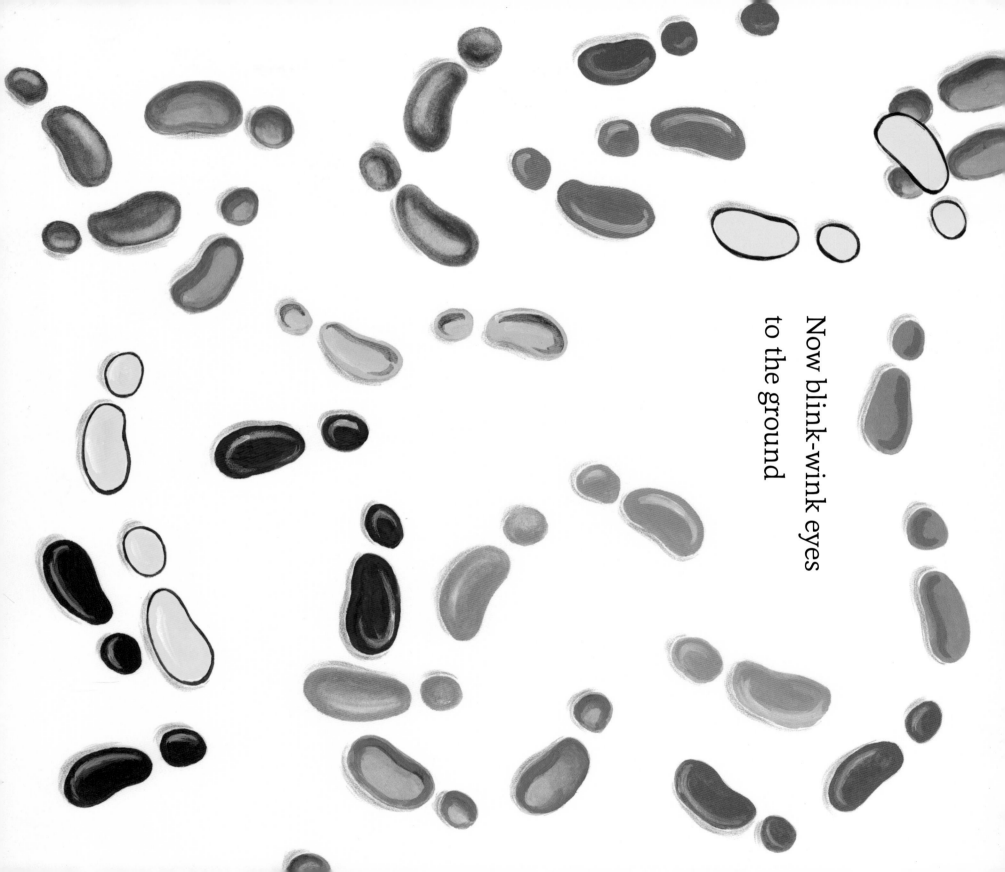

Now blink-wink eyes
to the ground

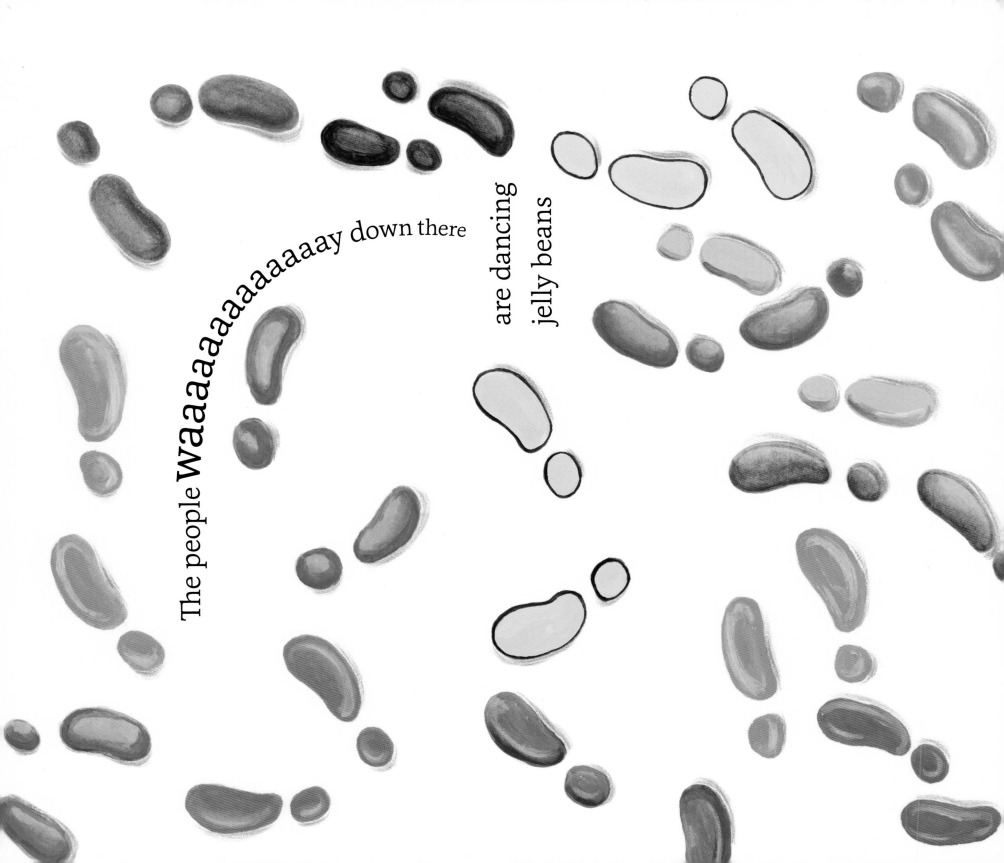

The people **Waaaaaaaaaaaaay** down there are dancing jelly beans

Strings of lights
slither in and out
zigzag
crisscross
in glowing
caterpillar rows

Hellooooooooo!

Mama, can you see us?

Mama, are you there?

Mama, aren't we brave,

flying waaaaaaaaaaaaaaaaaaaaaaaaaaaaaaay up here?

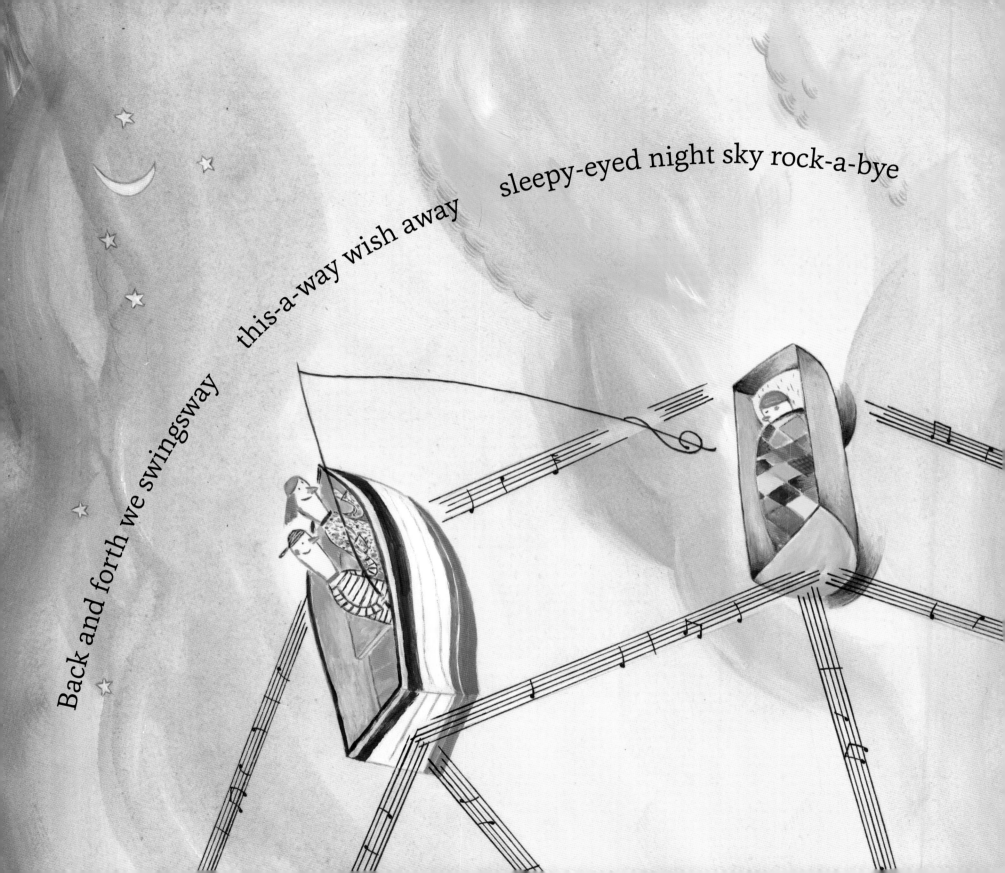

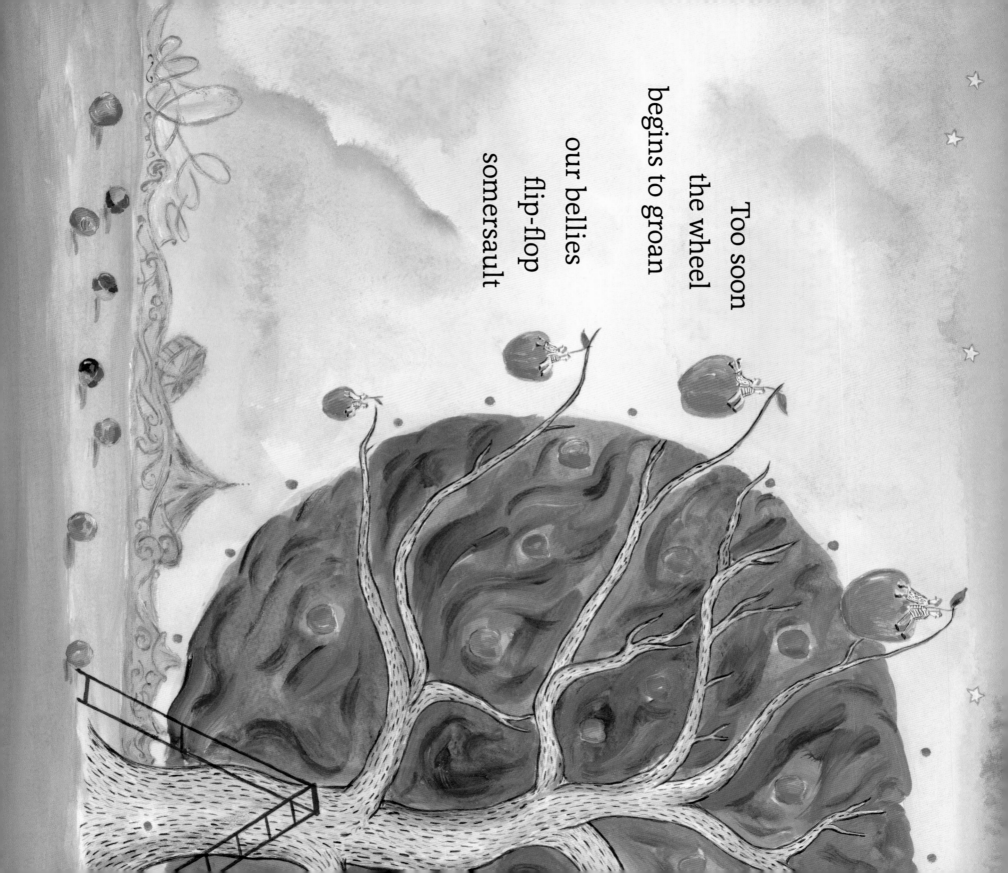

Too soon
the wheel
begins to groan

our bellies
flip-flop
somersault

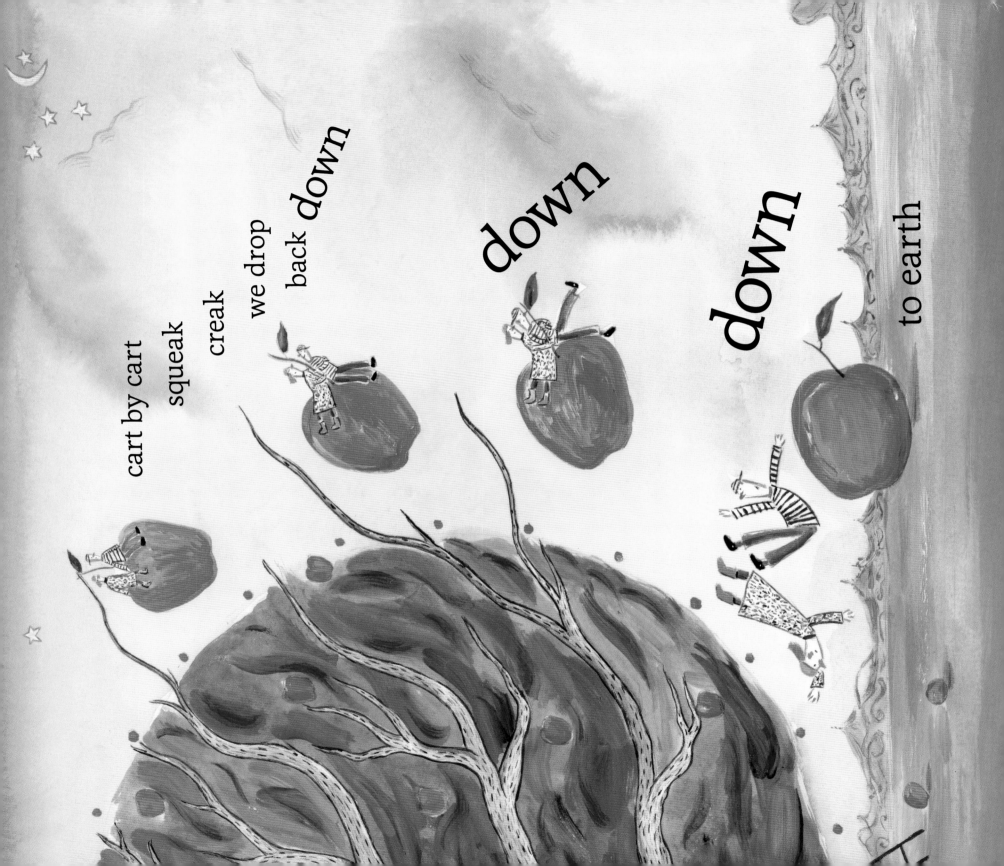

cart by cart

squeak

creak

we drop

back down

down

down

to earth

Mama, we did it! Mama, we flew!

Sister and Brother

mothers and fathers and all of the others

in the whole wide whirling world

We are fizzy with the dizzy reeling

fuzzy with the Ferris wheel feeling

Now and forever a part of the sky.

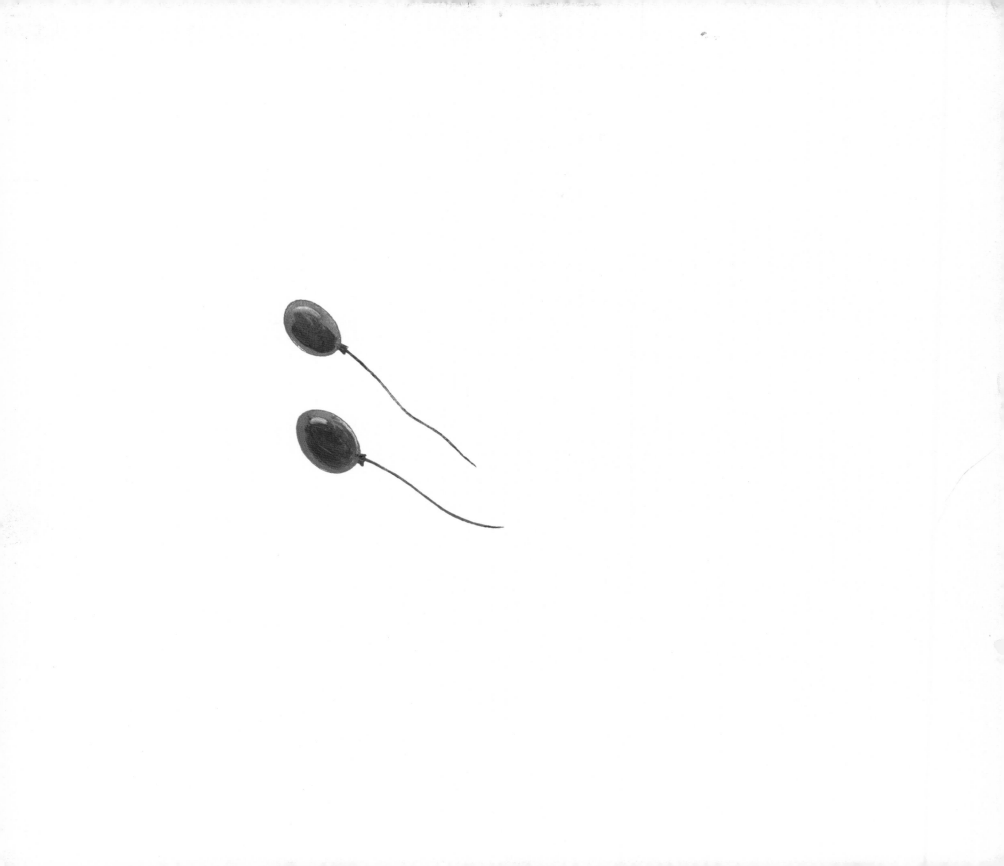

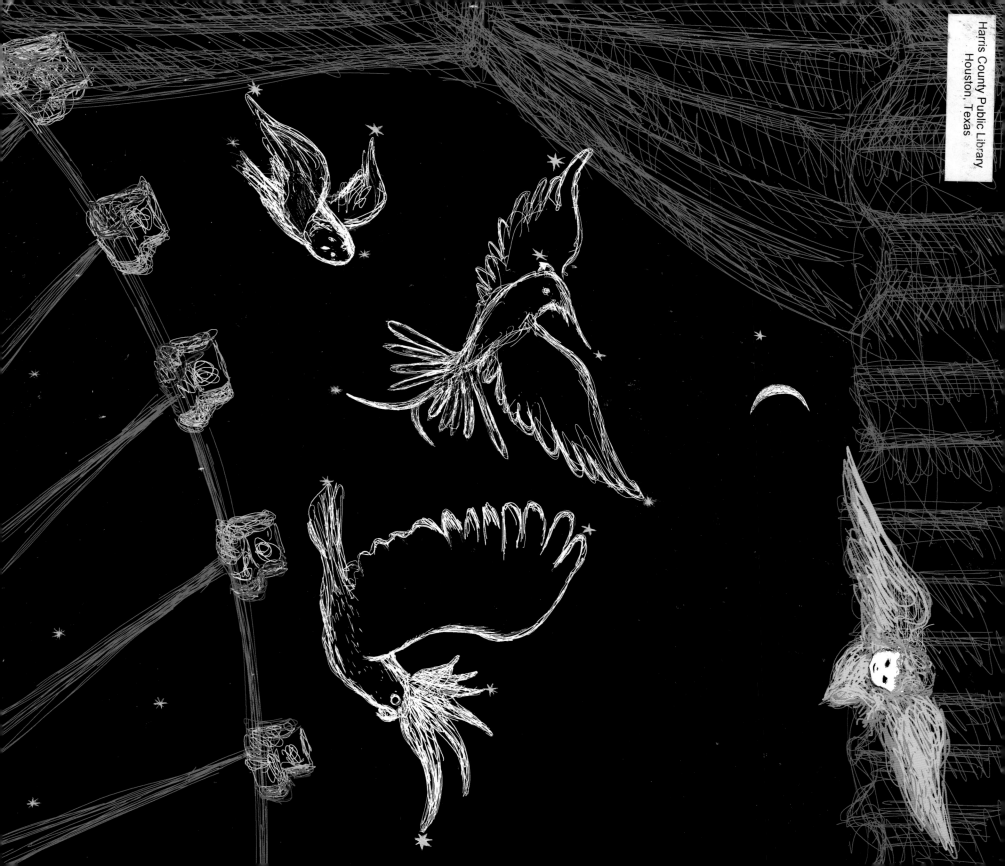